I0518230

CHILD OF THE STATION

MERCER TOOGOOD

Book design by Sage Gordon-Davis, MoonBunny Creative

Cover photos by Thom Schneider and Ann Agterberg via
unsplash.com

Dedicated to everyone that believed I could make it this far.

I made it.

THE SPACE STATION Atlas was unusually busy on the morning of the 40th day of the 517th year, and Frankie had nothing to do. It was Xaluvulax's Day, the last day of the Galactic Standard Week, meaning all the children that lived on board the Atlas got a day off from classes to relax and catch up on any missing work. But Frankie couldn't relax. Her parents always said she had been born without the ability to. She saw it as not wanting to waste her day.

She weaved through the crowds outside Port One, intrigued to see which ships had left and which had taken their places through the night. She saw a cargo crew moving their load onto a second ship, most likely to finish the journey. Most of the ships in the Beta Zephyrus Galaxy weren't allowed to leave the galaxy. The Council said it was for safety. Only those spaceships that were given a special designation were allowed to enter or leave the galaxy. Frankie didn't really understand why, but the law was the law.

She loved watching the space ships; loved trying to figure out where they were from and what they were carrying, if they were carrying anything. There was a ship with the symbol of the planet Nora 7J that was unloading crates of what looked like clothing, loading onto a ship that was going out of galaxy. Another, a passenger ship that had stopped over for the night before heading to the other side of the galaxy, was from X-789-01-C, the name of the solar system printed out in Frinoan.

She got to the Identification Barrier set up between the port and the rest of the Atlas, planting her Identification Card on the scanner. It beeped and turned green. The barrier opened for her, and she entered Port One. She milled about looking for something to do, staring at the different ships. The cargo ship from Nora 7J had just left, a cruise ship taking its place. The *CS Rotundra* was medium-sized, not even the largest cruise ship docked. *The Minxy* had been docked for four days now, planning on leaving at the twentieth hour to set a course for the Fireball Galaxy. Its captain was nice enough, but seemed to be wary of Frankie whenever she came near to say hi. Maybe it was just because he was an Uclian. They were a naturally skittish species, and looked like overgrown cockroaches.

She moved to the next ship, narrowing her eyes in contemplation. There was a battle cruiser that hadn't been there the night before. Spotting the name, she recognised it was one of the battle cruisers that patrolled around the galaxy and around the Atlas's Sister Stations. Captain Terik was Cordinian, like Frankie was, and always brought her some sweets from Cordan whenever he stopped there.

She'd never been to Cordan, the planet where her species had originated. She had been born on one of the Atlas's Sister Stations, the Atlas Epsilon. Her parents had told her stories about it, though; the sky was a light purple, a couple of shades lighter than Frankie's own skin was; the oceans were a deep blue, the grass a bright green; the twin suns that hung in the sky accompanied by twin moons. She'd grown up on stories about the moons chasing the suns, a game they'd played since their creation. She liked the story, but never really believed it to be true.

Someone bumped into her, knocking her out of her daze. She almost on the floor when the person grabbed her arm and stopped her from landing on her face. She pulled her arm out of the grip, turning around to see Xiv standing there, his face blushing a deep blue.

"Sorry, Franklin."

"How many times do I have to tell you to call me Frankie?" she asked him, looking up at his towering form.

He was the same age she was, thirteen, but Gnernoterans were known for their height and weight. They were a large species with four arms, pale blue skin, and a third eye planted in the middle of their forehead. Usually they were brutish and showed off their strength whenever they could, being the largest species originating in the X-231-14-F system, but Xiv was meek and shy. It might have been because he was raised in an orphanage. He'd only just been adopted by a Gnernoteran and brought to the Atlas Space Station four months ago.

"Sorry, Frankie. Sorry. I didn't see you there."

"It's fine," she said, swatting her hand at him. She remembered something, then, and narrowed her eyes in thought. "Shouldn't you be somewhere? Don't you usually have Station Training today?"

He nodded. "Yeah, but I took the day off today. I'm sick."

She crinkled her nose in disgust. "You don't look sick."

"I am. The tests told me so."

"I don't believe you."

"So what?" he asked. "I needed the day off, the class was stressing me out."

"It's mandatory for all new residents of the Atlas Space Station to go to Station Training to know how the station runs," she told him, crossing her arms over her chest.

"I'll make it up. It's just one day."

"It could be the most important lesson of the

class and you will have just missed it. If you don't go, I'm telling Station Security."

His eyes widened. "What?! Why would you do that?!"

"It's against the law to not go."

He stared at her for a second in disbelief. "Fine, I'll go! And you wonder why you don't have any friends."

He walked away, face creased in anger. A strange feeling entered Frankie's stomach, something she didn't recognise. It was like he had punched her in the gut, but he hadn't laid a finger on her. Her stomach

roiled, and she stuffed her hands into her pockets, bowed her head low to the floor, and started heading home.

After a few minutes of walking, just as she was taking her Identification Card out to have it scanned, she looked over her shoulder one last time. As she did, she saw two medium-sized cargo ships tucked into the corner of the Port, away from the rest of the ships. A Llotaidine was pulling cargo off the smaller ship, stamped with the insignia of the Yavurn 3 royal family, and loading it onto a Krean ship. The Krean that was supervising, a white skinned man with two arms, two legs, and a mop of black hair falling into his singular eye, was barking orders at the Llotaidine that was pushing the crate. She couldn't hear what he was saying from this distance, but the Llotaidine pushed harder. The box broke under his hands, and Frankie's eyes widened.

Inside the crate were plasma guns. From what Frankie remembered from history class, plasma guns had been outlawed when the war ended. She didn't even know they were still being made.

The Krean hit the Llotaidine over the head, spitting out something she couldn't understand. He shook his head before making the Llotaidine cover the crate with a tarp and continuing to loading the ship by himself.

She didn't know how long she was standing there, staring at the now covered weapons before the Krean made eye contact with her, his mouth turning into a deep scowl. He reached behind himself and pulled out a gun, identical to the ones in the crate, letting it rest next to his thigh. His eye didn't move from her the entire time he moved.

Her eyes widened and her heart skipped a beat as she moved as fast as she could, scanning her Identification Card before running out of sight of the Krean. As soon as she was out of his sight, she collapsed onto her knees in the middle of the thoroughfare. People started to cuss at her, but her legs wouldn't hold her anymore. Tears threatened to pour down her cheeks out of fright when a

Cordinian Station Security Officer, Officer Brolan, knelt down next to her and asked her what was wrong. She tried to explain, but when she opened her mouth, the only thing that came out were sobs.

"I'll comm your parents, Frankie," he told her.

She nodded, a couple of tears rolling down her cheeks as Officer Brolan spoke into his wristband, telling her parents that something had happened to her.

They were there in under three minutes.

Her mother sat down to her left, an arm wrapping around her waist, while her father crouched down in front of her. Both of them were Station Security, having worked for the Atlas Space Stations longer than Frankie had been alive. It was where they had met, and it was where they had fallen in love.

"Is everything okay, sweetie?" her mother asked her, running her free hand through her daughter's bright red hair. "What happened? Are you alright?"

She shook her head, and tried to point behind her. "I- I saw these men, in the back of the Port. I saw them loading up a cargo ship with plasma guns. A Krean saw me—he pulled a gun on me!"

Her father's eyes widened. "Are you sure?"

She nodded, wiping at her eyes.

"If they managed to port then they were let in by someone," her mother said, worry on her face.

"Unless they hid it," her father said. "If they are smugglers, and that's a big *if*, Adra, they wouldn't be so bold as to leave the weapons out for us to see in our routine sweep."

Adra gave him a surprised look. "Look at her, Dorai, she's terrified! Something happened to her."

They looked at each other for a second before Dorai nodded and spoke into the comm that was built into his wristband. "*All available personnel we have a possible Code Seven in Port One. I repeat, we have a possible Code Seven in Port One. Over.*"

"Brolan, keep Frankie away from the Ports until this is sorted out," Adra said, standing up.

Officer Brolan nodded. He grabbed Frankie's arm and helped her to her feet, not letting go as they walked away from Adra and Dorai, and away from the Ports. He didn't let go until they were in the Housing District, and even then, he didn't leave her until she was safely in her home.

FRANKIE WAS WATCHING her tablet in the living room when her parents came into the apartment, both of them agitated at something. Frankie couldn't help but think that something was her.

Adra sat down next to her on the couch, running a hand down her face. Dorai stepped into the kitchen and grabbed a drink from the fridge, not looking at his daughter.

"Before we start," Adra said slowly, "I just want to say that your father and I are happy you're okay. But we want to make sure that you saw what you think you saw."

As Dorai came over, Frankie's stomach started churning, a lump forming in her throat. Something had happened on the ship. Did they not find the crates? Did they, but they weren't filled with weapons like she thought?

"As you know," Dorai said, sitting on the coffee table opposite Frankie, "there is a disease borne in the blood of Cordinians, which causes us to see things that aren't there, and experience things differently than they actually happen, all while it rots us from the inside."

Frankie's mind whirled as he spoke. He was talking about the Silver Delusion, something they had told her about when she was a child. There was no cure, and it could be dormant in anyone, waking up and attacking its host at any random time.

"I'm not sick," she said, her hands digging into the sides of the tablet. "I saw the guns."

"We just need to make sure," Adra comforted her. "We didn't find any this time. We're giving *The Nomad* another check at the sixth hour, before they're scheduled to leave. But if the weapons aren't there, we're going to need to get you checked out."

She squeezed her eyes closed, shaking her head. "No. No! I'm not sick! I saw them!"

"Frankie—"

"No!"

She stood up and stormed to her room, slamming the steel door shut. She rested her back against it, and began to slowly sink to the floor, tears prickling at her eyes as she hugged her tablet to her chest.

She wasn't sick. She knew what she'd seen.

She heard her parents talking through the door, but she didn't care. They thought she was sick. They thought she was hallucinating the weapons, hallucinating the fact that the Krean had threatened her with a gun. She doubted they were even going to have a second check of the ship.

She'd have to show them. Show them the guns and the smuggling. She'd prove she wasn't sick.

Turning around, she tapped the screen of her tablet. Holding it up to the door, she saw through the metal and into the living room, where her parents were talking about something. She couldn't hear what they were saying, but subtitles showed up on screen next to them as they spoke, telling her that they were talking about getting her tested.

She tapped on the screen again, looking at the time. Minute thirteen of the fourth hour. She had just under two hours to get on that ship and find the weapons. A hundred and eighty-seven minutes, to be precise. And only a hundred and sixty-four once her parents left the living room.

PORT ONE WAS MORE crowded than it had been earlier that morning, with more ships docked and more people milling around. Frankie had managed to sneak out of the apartment once her parents left the living room, making her way through the long winding halls of the Atlas Space Station, towards the Port she had seen the smugglers use.

She was going to show her parents she didn't have the Silver Delusion. She wasn't sick. She would know if she was sick.

The scanner to Port One scanned Frankie's Identification Card. Once she was in the Port, she headed towards the back corner. She hid behind a stack of crates that was waiting to be loaded into a Cesian cargo ship. She peeked around the side to see if anyone was guarding the Krean ship, and she saw there was no one there. She smiled at her fortune, but as she came around the crates to go over to the ship, something stopped her.

Boarding a ship without permission was trespassing, and trespassing was illegal on the Atlas. It invaded people's privacy, and undermined their trust in the station. Frankie didn't want to break the law. She'd been taught her entire life that the law was there to protect people, and breaking it, for whatever reason, meant that you had to be punished. By going on to that ship, she would be doing the exact thing she had been taught not to do. That almost stopped her from boarding the Krean cargo ship.

Almost.

There were weapons on board the ship, hidden somewhere where her parents and the other Station Security Officers hadn't looked. Frankie was smaller, leaner, she could fit in spaces they couldn't. The thought of her finding the plasma guns and showing her parents they were wrong, wrong about the weapons and her being sick, spurred her forward.

Looking around to make sure no one was watching her, she boarded the ship.

The inside of the cargo ship was just as sleek as the outside, the walls and ceiling a steely grey, the floor a pure black. She hid behind a beam that was jutting out of the wall near the entrance to the ship, which closed automatically behind her. She pressed herself into the metal wall, hoping no one had heard the door open and close. After a minute of no one coming to investigate, she sighed a breath of relief.

She really hadn't chosen the right shoes for this mission. They were the standard station shoes given to everyone, and they liked to squeak. She slowly tiptoed out of her hiding place, stepping as carefully as she could. Her eyes scanned everything, from the vent at the bottom of the wall to the t-section at the end of the hall.

She narrowed her eyes at the vent. She'd be able to get through the opening, if she could take off the cover. She wasn't a fan of small spaces, but she'd do it if it meant she could to find the weapons they had hidden on the ship, and prove she wasn't sick.

She tiptoed to the vent and pried at the edges with her fingers, but it wouldn't loosen up. Noting the screws in the corners of the vent, she swore under her breath. She surveyed at her surroundings. There must be a screwdriver around here somewhere.

Frankie tiptoed away from the vent and down the hallway to the t-section. She stopped, peering down each hall, not sure which way to go. There were no navigational markers on the walls she could use to get around. Taking a chance, she turned left, hugging the wall as best she could, keeping her ears open for any sounds that would suggest someone was approaching her.

The hallway curved to the right, deeper into the cargo ship. She'd seen more vents, but all of them had been screwed shut, much like the first one. After about a minute of walking, the hallway ended in a closed door.

She approached it, and it opened by itself.

Slowly, she stuck her head through to see what was on the other side. It was a cafeteria. An empty cafeteria. The various sized tables and chairs were all empty, though that's not where she was looking. There were two other doors that led into the cafeteria, both of them Frankie assumed led further into the ship.

She stepped into the cafeteria, not sure which one she was going to pick. Her best guess as to where the weapons would be was the cargo hold, but that's where Station Security would have checked most thoroughly, so they were more than likely not there, unless they had moved it after the inspection.

But they must have expected to be searched, otherwise they would be in the cargo hold with the rest of the cargo. So it was most likely still hidden.

But where? In the hull of the ship, where most species can't reach? In the vents?

She decided to go through the second door.

It led to another hallway, this one lined with doors. They stayed shut as she passed, as they each had a scanner next to them. If she had to guess, this was where the crew slept. Frankie felt uneasy as she stalked the hall, her body tensed, waiting for anything to jump out at her.

One of the doors behind her slid open, and her entire body froze in panic. Her heart started beating erratically in her chest, her arms and legs felt weighted down.

Footsteps came, and they spurred her into motion.

As quickly and as quietly as she could, Frankie started forward, turning a corner and hiding beneath a table that was built into the wall. She pressed herself against the wall. Her heartbeat pounded so loudly she could feel it in her ears, and she was sure they could hear it too. She heard the footsteps get closer and closer, and then she saw the feet of the Llotaidine that had put the weapons on board just an hour prior.

The Llotaidine passed, and she let out a breath she didn't realise she was holding. She reached down and pulled her shoes off her feet—the squeaky rubber having almost given her away—and tied the laces together, hanging them around her neck. In her socks, she got out from under the table and went back down the hall she had just come from, hoping to keep the Llotaidine behind her.

Back in the cafeteria, the first door led to another hallway, this one with far fewer doors. The ones she came across didn't have scanners next to them, instead having plaques written in Krel. Frankie couldn't read Krel, and the translator she had didn't account for the written word. It didn't matter, though. She searched through every single one, looking for signs of the weapons.

The seventh room she entered was different from the rest. While they had been used for storage or extra holdings of cargo, this one was almost completely bare, with the few crates that were in it pressed against the wall next to the door. The opposite wall had been opened up, several metal panels strewn across the floor, and there were sounds coming from the hole in the wall.

"I just don't get why we have to take it out *now*," someone snarled. "We're just gonna have to put it back once we reach *The Mynnervaa*."

Someone else sighed, sounding exasperated. "Look, you're new here, so I'll give you the benefit of the doubt. We can't move when there's something in the hull because it destabilises the ship.

We hide it in here so Station Security don't find it, but then we have to move it out before we leave."

"Can't we just get a better ship?"

"It's not as simple as that, Axl-874."

Something grabbed the back of Frankie's shirt, lifting her off her feet. A screamed ripped from her throat as she thrashed, trying to break free. She clawed at the arm holding her as she was turned around, and she was shoved right in the face of a Gnernoteran.

"I knew I smelled something gross on the ship," he growled into her face. Fear coursed through her veins as the Gnernoteran grinned, baring his toothy maw. "Captain Botar-3 wants to see you."

FRANKIE WAS CARRIED through the halls of *the Nomad* by the Gnernoteran, who refused to let her go. They wound through the cargo ship, Frankie's fear making her not pay attention to where they were going. All she knew was that all the halls looked the same, and she was about to be in a lot of trouble.

They got to the Captain's quarters, the Gnernoteran knocking loudly on the door. Someone inside told them to come in, and they entered. The Gnernoteran threw Frankie onto the ground, her palms and knees hitting the metal floor hard, and she hissed in pain as they throbbed.

"We've got a stowaway," the Gnernoteran explained.

The feet in front of her turned, and a snarl sounded above her.

"No, she's not," said the man Frankie assumed was Captain Botar-3. "She's the one that saw us loading the plasma guns."

She looked up at him, and she saw the Krean that had seen her staring earlier looking down at her with one big white eye, the iris a deep brown and blending in with the pupil. There was a scar she didn't see earlier, running down the left side of his face from his hairline, crossing over his mouth, and running down into the collar of his shirt. There was a scowl on his face, showing yellowed teeth. The fear in her grew as another growl escaped his throat.

But despite the fear and the dread that were filling her, she also felt relief. There *were* weapons on board. She *wasn't* sick.

"What do we do with her?"

The Captain narrowed his eye at her, contemplating what he should do. "Call Station Security. Let them know someone broke onto the ship."

"But what about the weapons? She overheard Axl-874 and Kriilag talking about them."

"They're not going to believe her, not after she broke the law."

The Gnernoteran grunted, and footsteps faded behind her as he left, but she couldn't stop staring at the single eye of the Krean. It hadn't left her body since she had been thrown at his feet.

"What are you doing on my ship?" Captain Botar-3 demanded.

She swallowed the bile rising in her throat, the fear coursing through her stopping her from talking. Her mouth hung open limply, and she was frozen to the floor on all fours, not even noticing the pain in her knees.

"You thought you could find the plasma guns yourself?" He scoffed. "You're a child. How are you going to do something Station Security couldn't?"

"I—" She stopped, feeling like she was going to vomit.

"They're going to come for you, and you're going to be in a lot of trouble for trespassing. And because of that, they're going to let us deport early. So, I do have to thank you, Cordinian. In trying to stop us, you've inadvertently helped us."

She threw up all over his shoes, making him jump in disgust and take a few steps back.

Despite her lightheadedness from the fear and the vomiting, Frankie managed to push herself to her feet and sprint out of the room. She heard

Captain Botar-3 shout after her as she ran. Her ears were ringing as she ran, and she heard the Captain's voice ring out over her through the intercom system:

"The Cordinian is escaping! Don't let her leave the ship!"

Frankie ran as fast as she could through the halls of *The Nomad*, wishing she had paid attention to the path the Gnernoteran had taken her down. At the moment, she was going down every hall she could, trying to get as much distance between her and the Krean Captain.

A small Sinoid came skidding out of a side room, each of its six arms on it's one-foot body holding a knife about half as long as they were. Frankie managed to jump over the Sinoid and turn a corner, hearing its wings flapping behind her.

There were several shouts throughout the cargo ship as she weaved through the hallways, guessing where she was going. She was sure she was going around in circles, as she saw the same table set into the wall again and again. But she didn't care. She needed to find the weapons and then get out before the crew caught her, which was proving more difficult than she thought it would be.

She ran down another corridor and through the door at the end, running right into the cafeteria. She sighed in relief as she realised she knew where she was going now. She took one of the other doors leading to the room she had found earlier, counting out to the seventh room. She entered the room, the panels half covering the hole in the wall, several crates of weapons stacked up next to the normal boxes of cargo.

Frankie ran to the still-opened crate that had been broken while being loaded and grabbed for the first thing she could. She wrapped her fingers around the cool metal of the gun and brought it out; it was a pistol. She wasn't sure what to do with it: she'd never held a gun before. Doing what she had seen Captain Botar-3 do about two hours earlier, she reached behind her and tucked the pistol into the back of her pants, and turned around to leave.

Only to see a Uclian standing in the doorway, a clicking sound coming out of its mandibles. It held a plasma gun at her and, saying something in a language her translator wouldn't translate, pulled the trigger.

FRANKIE DOVE for the hole in the wall as the Uclian pointed the plasma gun at her, but she was too slow. The plasma bolt hit her leg, blasting her backwards. She slammed into the metal wall, the edge of the hole digging into her stomach as the momentum carried her over the side. She felt blood seeping through her shirt as she fell head-first into the hull. She started screaming, her leg burning from the pain of being shot with a plasma bolt.

She didn't want to look at it, in fear that it would make it worse. But she could feel where her flesh had been ripped off, could feel the blood pumping out of her leg through the wounds it had made, could feel it travelling down her upside-down body, coating her clothes in the vile black liquid.

The world became fuzzy around her as the edges of her vision blackened and tears ran up her face. She was in the small area between the outside of the ship and the inside, to help stop the pressure of space from crushing spaceships mid-flight. It wasn't much, but it helped.

But that small space was making her heart race, panic racing through her veins as the wounds on her leg and stomach made her want to pass out, her claustrophobia stopping her from breathing properly in the tiny space she had found herself in.

She could hear the Uclian calling out for some-one, but the pounding in her ears made it impos-sible to figure out what. There were banging sounds, and then something grabbed at the leg that had been shot. A scream ripped out of her throat as she was lifted up by it, the Sinoid carrying all her weight through it.

She must have blacked out for a minute, because the next thing she remembered she was lying on the floor of the cargo ship, staring up at the metallic ceiling. She tried to sit up, but the Gnernoteran was holding her down as a Niadpir poked and prodded at her leg, Captain Botar-3 watching as he stood over her, arms crossed.

"Station Security will be here any second," he told her, looking at her wounded leg. "I've commed them and told them we need medical assistance as well."

She wanted to say something, but the Niadpir stuck her finger in the wound, touching the bone, and she threw up onto the floor next to her.

The Niadpir chuckled awkwardly. "Sorry."

She faintly heard footsteps in the hall outside the room, and four Station Security Officers appeared in the open doorway, led by the Sinoid that had lifted her from the hull. The Security Officers looked surprised when they saw Frankie lying on the floor.

Two Station Medics came through the door after them, a stretcher between them. One of them, a Cordinian with dark purple skin, asked the Niadpir and Gnernoteran to take a step back. They did, and the Medics placed the stretcher on the floor next to her. The second Medic, a Krean, wrapped something around Frankie's leg. She wasn't sure what it was, but she knew it felt a lot better once she had secured it around her leg. They then moved her onto the stretcher, Frankie letting out a painful squeal.

Frankie reached for where the crates full of weapons were, to show the Security Officers. But when she looked to see where they were, they were gone. She looked at the hole in the wall, but that had been fully covered, too. She narrowed her eyes in confusion, the pain in her leg causing her not to think straight.

"The weapons were there," she said, pointing at the wall. "They were in the hull, I saw them."

"I'm going to need you to take a deep breath," the Cordinian Medic told her, lowering something over her mouth.

She shook her head, the room spinning as she did. Whatever he was giving her was already working. She pointed at the hull wall, trying to say something through the mask, but not even she could figure out what she was trying to say. She reached up to try and pull the thing off her mouth, but she was weak, and moving was painful.

She tried to point at the hull one more time,

but as the darkness came done on her, swallowing her in its cold embrace, she felt her arm go limp.

FRANKIE WOKE up in the Medical District of the Atlas Space Station, a place she'd been to only a handful of times before. The window was facing the closest stars, Phe A and Phe B, the natural light streaking over her as she laid in the bed.

She looked around. It wasn't often she saw the stars' light in the station. Her home was in the central column of the Atlas, and she had no windows. It was the same with her classrooms. The only times she really saw their light was while she was wandering through the Ports, or the places the tourists went to. Which were only on her days off, and she didn't get many.

She tried to sit up in bed to get a better look at the stars, the glass coated with a special layer of protection to stop the harmful rays from entering the station, but a jagged pain in her stomach made her gasp out.

"You're awake," a familiar voice said.

It took her a second to realise it was her mother's voice. She looked to the other side to see her sitting there, her father sound asleep and snoring lightly next to her, fist propped up against his cheek. Adra whacked him on the chest, and he flinched awake. He looked around for a second, confused, but his eyes widened when he saw his daughter.

"You're awake!" he said, grinning. He stood up and leaned down to give her a hug, but Adra whacked him again. "Ow! What was that for?"

"She's in pain, Dorai, don't hurt her even more," she told him. He grumbled, but sat back down.

One of the Medics, obviously hearing the commotion, approached the bed. It was the Cordinian that had helped Frankie on *The Nomad*. He started doing tests and checks on her, poking and prodding her body.

"How are you feeling?" he asked as he shined a light in her eyes. "Sore," she said. "Can you lift up my bed? I want to see the stars."

"In a minute. I'm sure your parents would like to know how this happened."

Adra nodded. "We really would. I thought we told you we were going to do another check of the ship before they left?"

Frankie shook her head. "You wouldn't have found the weapons. They were hiding them in the hull of the ship."

Dorai's brows shot to his hairline. "They'd risk compromising their hull just so they can smuggle things?" He shook his head. "The things people will do for money."

"But why did you go looking for them?" Adra asked, brow furrowed in worry.

Frankie stayed silent for a moment, feeling tears prickle at her eyes. "I didn't want to be sick."

"Oh, honey," she said, hand to her chest.

"You're lucky you found them," Dorai told her. "If it wasn't for the gun you had put in your pants —which is *very dangerous*, don't *ever* do that again —we would've had to let them go because of the crime that you had committed on their ship. But because of the gun, we had cause to search it again. I'll tell Foreman Zovill-710 to look in the hull for the rest of them."

"What happened to the crew?" she asked him.

"They're all being held in custody," Adra told her. "Once we find the rest of the smuggled weapons, we'll be able to arrest them and send them to Okra-9. I'm proud of you, Frankie."

Dorai nodded. "We both are."

Frankie couldn't stop the grin that was growing on her face. Her efforts hadn't been in vain. She had managed to stop the crew of *The Nomad*, stop Captain Botar-3.

"Let me lift your bed up for you," the Cordinian Medic said, pressing a button on the side of the bed.

The front of the bed slowly started rising, the stars slowly coming into view of the window. She closed her eyes and tilted her head towards the stars as she basked in their light. The dual star system stood out against the myriad of stars and galaxies in the distance: even the smaller one was larger than the entire Space Station she had lived on for most of her life.

Every time she saw the Phe Sisters, she thought about how small and insignificant she was; how if she hadn't been born, not much would change. And she had been fine with that.

But after what had happened on the Krean cargo ship, she wasn't sure that was true anymore. Sure, it wasn't a lot, but those guns she had found in the hull of *The Nomad* wouldn't be used to hurt people like they would have if she didn't interfere.

And as she looked out at the stars, she realised that maybe she did belong among them. Every star that shone in the sky was important, so why not every soul that lived and died and *yearned* for more, to *be* more?

She held her parents' hands in hers, and together they watched the stars.

ACKNOWLEDGMENTS

Firstly, I'd like to acknowledge the writing communities that kept me writing when I felt like giving up. My friends on Twitch, YouTube, and (formerly) Wattpad, you have helped me through many, many, *many* bouts of the dreaded Writer's Block, and I thank you for that.

To my family, to Danelle, Alan, Joshua, Nanna, Aunty Cath, Uncle Anthony, Aaron, and Levi, who have been there for me during my writing, and have let me talk their ears off about ideas I was passionate about, but ultimately ended up abandoning. You kept me from going crazy.

To my friends, Luke and Simone, who know just how deep into my writings I get. They watched me as I wrote in classes, only just scraping by in high school. Thank you for telling me to do my work every now and then, because if you didn't, I wouldn't have my diploma.

To my English teachers, sorry for forgetting your names. You've taught me a lot about proper grammar and punctuation, and how to properly use a semicolon; sorry for throwing some of those rules away to make the sentences smoother. It was necessary.

But most important of all: to my sister, Caitlin, who got me into writing in the first place. If it wasn't for you, I may not have found my passion at all, and definitely not as early as I did. Writing helped me through a tough time in my life, and I'm all the better for it. This book wouldn't be here if you didn't start it all, so I thank you for also wanting to write a book. I hope it all works out for you.

ABOUT THE AUTHOR

Mercer Toogood is a genderfluid writer living outside the city of Perth with their aunt, uncle, and cousin. They have been writing on and off since they were about ten, but only really started properly when they hit high school. They started off writing fanfiction, and still does mostly write it, but decided to write an original. After struggling for several years trying to write a novel, they realised they could write short stories with ease. As their first book, and also their first foray into Science Fiction, they are excited to share their writing to the world.